Kartik

Kartik's War

Subhadra Sen Gupta

Rupa . Co

Published 2002 by

Rupa • Co

7/16, Ansari Road, Daryaganj,
New Delhi 110 002

Sales Centres:

Allahabad Bangalore Chandigarh Chennai
Dehradun Hyderabad Jaipur Kathmandu
Kolkata Ludhiana Mumbai Pune

Commissioning Editor: Paro Anand
Cover Design: Tapas Guha

ISBN 81-7167-875-0

Typeset in 11 pts Caxton by
Nikita Overseas Pvt Ltd,
1410 Chiranjiv Tower,
43 Nehru Place,
New Delhi 110 019

Printed in India by
Saurabh Print-O-Pack
A-16, Sector IV, NOIDA 201 301

For my Nephew and old Friend Arijit Sen
Finally A Book Exclusively for you
With Love

Contents

Contents

Chapter One

A New Job for Kartik

I did not really believe that Lord Shiva would listen to me. He is a busy god after all, and among all the usual prayers for money and children, marriage and sickness, my request was, to be honest, quite odd.

I tried to put myself in Lord Shiva's place—sitting there, bathed in Ganga water and milk, with people throwing flowers and *bael* leaves at him, yelling out their prayers, chanting mantras, ringing the bells, arguing with the priests. And in all this noise and confusion, I come up and mutter my prayer.

I can imagine him sitting up and frowning, "What did you say, my son?"

"Won't you please start a war, dear Lord?"

"What is it that you said you wanted? A jar? A chariot car?"

"No no. A war. Fighting battles, the king leading out an army…"

"Don't be ridiculous. No one prays to start wars. To win them after they have started it, yes. But not start one. Especially now? And to tell the truth, I can't risk it, my son. If the king found out it started with my blessings, he could close down this temple. Y'know the mood he is in… and I'd be out of business…"

"You mean you are refusing the prayers of a devotee? A true *bhakta* for twenty years?"

"Go to Durga, son. She is the goddess of war, and like all women, enjoys taking risks. She's not afraid of anyone at all. Quite reckless, as a matter of fact. She will oblige, I'm sure."

Standing there in a jostling crowd of devotees at the door of the Shiva temple, I grinned to myself. In Ashoka's kingdom even mad, old Shiva was getting nervous of war and if the gods were getting the jitters, could I blame the humans for turning into peace loving citizens to save their skins? But then, who could I turn to? Ashoka's new favourites, those saffron-clad, bell-ringing monks would definitely not be interested in my plans.

I think I should explain what all this is about before you get completely confused and stop listening to me. And friend, this is a story worth listening to, especially over an excellent cup of wine.

My name is Kartik—in the Hindu pantheon, he is the general of the army of gods. Sort of an appropriate name for me, I think. Actually, my parents optimistically named me Kartikendu Vardhan, as if the royal touch to my name would make me a prince. Well, it never works that way, does it? So I became what my father was and his father before him. I followed the family profession and I became a royal spy. A spy employed in the army of King Ashoka Vardhan of Pataliputra, of the Maurya clan—the unquestioned monarch of the kingdom of Magadha.

Do not look so amused. It is an honourable profession and for the safety of a kingdom, a very essential one. Now there are two kinds of spies—one who keeps an eye on things within the kingdom, spots rebellions, discovers criminals planning to rob the king's treasury, kidnap a prince, that sort of thing. I did not do that kind of low level, internal drudgery. I belonged to the elite of the fraternity, I was a military spy and we are at our best when the king is going on an expedition or a conquest or facing an invasion. When we infiltrate the enemy forces and try to discover their plans. The king may not admit to it but he gets reports from us, spies, many times in a day. We are his eyes and ears across the kingdom.

I grew up listening to the tales of adventure of my grandfather who had served under the great Chandragupta, our king's grandfather and the founder of this kingdom. Now, that was a real man! Magadha was then ruled by the dynasty of the Nandas, a weak, corrupt clan that had forgotten the duties of the throne and were only interested in their own debauched lives. Then Chandragupta came, like a bolt of lightning, and defeated the last Nanda king. Beside him, all through the years of struggle, was his Brahmin guru and mentor, Chanakya. Legend says, Chanakya was once insulted by the Nandas and took his revenge by discovering Chandragupta from nowhere and creating a great general and king out of him. During all these years of war, my grandfather was with them and when the triumphant Mauryan army entered Pataliputra, he was right there in the first group of horsemen.

My father served Chandragupta's son, King Bindusara and I was proud to join the royal army when I was old enough. Things were good in the beginning. Ashoka was building an empire and was perennially hungry for land. We were conquering the kingdoms, one after the other. I saw action in the south beyond the Narmada river, up north in the foothills of the Himalayas and towards the kingdom of Taxila. Those were great days—going into strange cities in disguises, checking out the movement of the armies, finding traitors in the enemy camp and running them along with other spies. I would cross borders like smoke and vanish into crowded city lanes. Ashoka trusted me then and I could reach him anytime of the day and night because, at his orders, I had unquestioned entry into the royal palace. I could even walk into his bed chamber and no one would stop me. Ah! Those were the good old days.

Then Kalinga ruined everything. This southern kingdom had been coveted by Magadha for years because it offered the easiest access to the sea and we needed it for our growing trade. But the Kalinga army was famed for its valour, and even this time, though completely outnumbered by Ashoka's forces, they fought with unbelievable courage. It was the most ferocious battle I have ever seen. They say over a hundred thousand lay dead at the end, creating villages and towns of widows. This was a battle where there was no winner, we had lost too much. The funeral pyres burnt for weeks and every home in Pataliputra seemed to be in mourning.

Standing there in the battlefield, looking at the devastation that he had caused, Ashoka underwent a rapid change. He vowed not to fight another war of aggression again. I can understand his feelings. For a while after Kalinga, we all found it unbearable to think of war but, to be frank, I did not think his resolve would last. It was so unlike the Ashoka we knew. He was too ambitious, with grandiose plans of ruling an empire, too good a general, and I knew that since he was a teenager he had enjoyed the challenge of war strategy and the heat of a battle. And who had ever heard of a king giving up war after winning one? But he surprised all of us. Magadha declared peace forever, and I was out of a job.

So, as a last ditch effort, here I was mumbling my prayers to Lord Shiva. Then after shoving a few coins into the ever-waiting palm of the greedy eyed priest, I pushed my way out of the temple crowd. Coming out into the street, I wandered down Pataliputra's main bazaar. Past the flower shops and the shacks selling trinkets and brass *puja* utensils to the pilgrims, the row of beggars and sweet shops where the cooks were already sweating over huge cauldrons of boiling milk. It was still quite early in the morning and the clothes and jewellery shops were only beginning to open their doors. The shopkeepers were dusting their shelves and sweeping their floors, sprinkling water on the threshold and lighting incense before their idols of Goddess Lakshmi. Mallika should have arrived, too, by now.

Mallika has a small arcade near the bazaar's most popular food shop where she sells *paan*, that addictive mixture of lime and areca nut, essences and spices wrapped up like a love potion in a betel leaf. Mallika makes a wide array of *paans* and adds to them those heady glances from her kohl lined eyes and her laughing, flirtatious chatter. She is a very popular lady. This morning as I strolled up to her shop, she gave me a sharp look and then went on laying out her silver salvers and bowls, "Kartik, busy as usual, I see! Where are you coming from at such an unearthly hour?"

"Went to the temple. Thought Shiva may agree to start a war."

She curved her glance upwards, "Did he?"

I shook my head. "Do you think Durga or Kali may oblige?"

She laughed. "But I thought you had been given a new job by the king. Haven't you started working yet?"

"Sure. He wants me to join the team of internal spies. Me doing such work!"

"Why not. What's wrong with it? Spying is spying. And you know no other kind of work. What will you do instead, sell bananas in the market?"

That comment about bananas was really unfair. "Can you imagine me checking out rebellions in some god forsaken province and keeping track of burglars?"

"Quite easily. Work is work."

I sighed. "Ah well. Will you marry me if I joined up?"

"I would think about it. Right now you are not even worth thinking of as a suitor. I don't want to spend my life listening to those endless stories of your military heroics. And what's wrong with catching criminals anyway?"

Nothing's wrong with it, nothing at all. So to keep her happy, I wandered down the bazaar to the office of my new boss, Sarvaka, the chief of the internal spy department. I entered the antechamber of his office and reported in. His personal assistant, sitting cross-legged before a low table, looked up from a pile of official looking leaf manuscripts and pointed his quill pen to the door. "He wants to see you immediately. Some urgent job."

"Urgent? What's up? Someone's attacked the kingdom?"

The man gave a crooked smile and said with a patient sigh, "This is not the army, my friend. And there is no war. Stop dreaming."

Everyone is giving me advice these days.

I sidled into Sarvaka's room. It was, as always, busy with people. An assistant stood waiting to take away a pile of official orders, two spies were being given instructions on their next job, a writer was taking down dictation. Sarvaka sat in the middle of it on his divan, like a benign despot, the low table before him strewn with reports. He was a large man, both in height and width, that is. I have heard he was a retired wrestler and if he was, then he was a rare one because this man was no lowbrowed muscle man, he had a sharp, pitilessly analytical mind behind that thick featured dark face. And for all his habit of smiling smoothly, not benign at all. I had been in the room often when he reported to Ashoka. He was precise, well informed and quick in his thinking. You couldn't fool him easily. So I was careful about what I said, and even harder for me, I was polite.

He waved me to a seat and, to my surprise, asked everyone else to leave the room. As he leaned back against a bolster, I sat up.

"His Highness has requested that you be taken on as a *cara*, first class in my department." He sighed gustily as if Ashoka had been unreasonable. "He insisted."

"I was already a military *cara* first class, so it's not a promotion." I informed him. In the royal records, a *cara* is a spy.

"I know. But you have no experience of internal work. It requires a different expertise. You have to know the area, develop sources of information. It takes years of work. I do not know what kind of work I can offer you."

Ah, so our friend Sarvaka did not like it either. A man like me could easily ruin the discipline of his department. I was too experienced, I had always operated alone and reported straight to the generals or the king. For Sarvaka, I spelled trouble. But Mallika's words rang in my head, I needed this job. So I looked obedient and uncharacteristically helpful.

"I am familiar with Pataliputra, sir, and I have many sources in the city already in place, especially in the army and among the foreign embassies. I could begin here. And, sir," I put the respectful bit in again deliberately, "if I can gather information in enemy territory, my own city shouldn't pose much of a problem."

"The king also said I should allow you to choose your assignments."

Ah! Bless him, Ashoka never missed a trick. I stayed silent.

"He also said, I should be careful, you like being heroic, you are rebellious and troublesome like an unbroken horse, and for my own peace of mind, I should let you operate alone."

Sarvaka's face had the sour look of a man sucking a lemon. He reached for some leaf pages lying before him and said, "So I have a choice of three jobs, you pick what you like."

I leaned forward, trying to look eager. "A theft in the house of a minister." I faintly shook my head.

"The kidnapping for ransom of the son of a businessman

who has complained to the palace that the police is not doing anything."

I gave a noncommital shrug.

"Complaints about a bureaucrat working in the palace that he is taking bribes." Sarvaka's voice took on the official ring as he read out. "That he 'possesses property disproportionate to his known sources of income'. You will have to find evidence that he does have such property and then provide proof that he is taking bribes. The second part is usually impossible to prove unless you can catch him red-handed after a complaint or someone gives evidence against him with proof."

Very encouraging.

I thought for a while and chose the last one. If I had expected any reaction from my new boss, I was disappointed. Looking businesslike as usual. Sarvaka briefed me. The order for investigation had come from Minister Sripala, who headed the Department of Civil Supplies. This bureaucrat, Ramadatta worked in Sripala's department as a writer of orders. He was a middle level bureaucrat who sat in the palace and earned a middle level salary. Recently, he had been displaying sudden signs of wealth.

"Remember this is just a watching brief, Kartik. Follow the man around, check out his visitors, discover the opportunities to take bribes." Sarvaka's voice took on the deep echo of a warning. "But I don't want you to take any action without clearing it with me or Minister Sripala. We cannot anger a bureaucrat, they have a very strong organisation. Do not play a hero and try to arrest him. Use your head and don't get excited. One has to step carefully in such matters. Do you understand me?"

I kept nodding and then said, "Looks easy. Don't worry, sir. You'll have your answer in a week."

As always, I spoke too early. Sarvaka gave me a doubtful glare as he dismissed me and I sauntered out again. Easy job. So easy I decided to give myself a holiday and start it the following day.

Next day I decided to reach the palace early because before I began my watch I had some work with an old friend, Kaushik, who was the captain of the palace guards. When I left my home, the sun was still a soft glow in the sky and the roads were deserted. My house is on the outskirts of the city and as Ashoka's palace is in the heart of Pataliputra, it is a long way, but the weather was so pleasant, I decided to walk instead of hailing a horse cart.

I like Pataliputra at dawn, before the crowds take over. I strolled along the narrow road running beside the city's outer walls that at times follow the path of the Ganga river. Huge tree trunks piled in a solid row make the invincible palisade that guards the city, and to make things even harder for an invading army, there is that dirty moat on the other side. Once when I was standing near the king, I heard Ashoka joke that during a siege, all you needed was to make the enemy drink the moat water and we would have won. I looked up to the ramparts. The guards marching around on top keep vigil all night at the watch towers. With a lot of creaking of bolts the big gateway was being swung open to let in the rows of bullock carts bringing supplies into town—bags of wheat and rice,

mountains of vegetables and fruits, spices, cloth, pottery...
Pataliputra was a hungry city.

I went through the narrow, winding, dusty lanes of the
poorer parts of the city, with low thatched or tiled roof
houses and open sewers. Then the closer I got to the centre
of the town the nicer the view became. There were trees
beside the road, parks with ponds and pavilions. The road
was now cobbled and the houses were many stories high
with gardens, outhouses, wells, and porticos where the
carriages stood. I went past a public bathing pool already
full of people. The vegetable market was bustling with
buyers and sellers bent over the peas and beans and women
bargaining for the cucumbers and bananas.

Standing outside Ashoka's palace I looked up to the
ramparts and the triumphant flags flying over the watch
towers. At the gate, the mounted troops who guarded it were
not too keen to let me in but I carried Sarvaka's order. Also,
I said, I was going to meet their boss, so the tiny door set
in the gate was swung open to let me in. Kaushik as head
of the palace guards has his office right next to the main
gateway. When I arrived, he welcomed me with his usual
resigned calm, like a patient adult handling a willful child.
Nothing stays secret in the palace for long, so he knew all
about my new job even before I got to him and my request
did not surprise him at all.

Kaushik and I know each other's working methods well.
I have used him for information many times before because
he has a great network of informants, the most obvious of
all—his guards. There they stand at the doors and gates,
silent and forgotten but behind their impassive faces their

ears and eyes are hard at work. And they report everything to their boss. Another great source of gossip is the captain of the charioteers. His men drive the palace officials and royal men around in chariots and carriages and hear everything. People can be remarkably careless before silent people like servants, guards, eunuchs and drivers.

Kaushik allowed me to borrow a guard's uniform and gave me a false assignment. I put on the stitched, short sleeved guard's tunic over my *antariya*, tied a scarlet sash around my waist. Then I knotted my long hair, which I usually leave free, into a guard's head band and tied a jaunty knot over one ear. Kaushik looked me over with an amused smile and said I looked stupid enough to be a guard at a bureaucrat's door.

Leaving Kaushik's office I walked through the outer palace. Ashoka's palace has an outer public area and after a row of gates the inner private area where the king's personal quarters and the harem are located. One has to go through a maze of courtyards with rooms all around. In this public area there are stables, cowsheds, and elephant stalls. The king even has his private aviary and animals. I went past the granaries and the coach houses for the royal carriages and palanquins.

The beautiful wooden pavilion, with intricately carved and lacquered pillars, where dancers and musicians perform for the public was now deserted. After crossing important offices, like the treasury and the political departments, closer to the king's personal quarters, I reached the outer offices of bureaucrats and marched up to the door of Ramadatta's office and stood straight, holding my spear, carefully keeping my face impassive and doing my best to act like a real guard on duty.

The guard at the next office gave a curious stare and asked, "I haven't seen you before. Are you sure you have been assigned to that door? Usually, I manage both these offices."

"You can check with the captain." I said shortly.

Curious people can be the biggest headache for spies trying to look inconspicuous. But our friend wasn't going to give up easily. He looked me up and down and then commented, "You don't look like a guard. When did you join the services?"

"This morning." Learning from experience, I keep my lying to the minimum.

"And the captain gave you duties right inside the palace on your first day?"

"I know a minister or two. It helps."

"Ah, that it does. I spent the first four years guarding the palace walls. You are lucky. Did you have to pay anyone to get this special duty?"

I had a feeling my upright friend Kaushik would not be pleased at the direction the conversation was going. I shook my head. "You know the captain, he is not like that."

Then the officials began to arrive and the man moved away. I sighed with relief and got busy trying to spot my quarry, the bureaucrat Ramadatta. I can spot a bureaucrat from miles away. There is this look of self importance, and the sauntering, lazy style of moving, as if the whole world will wait for their pleasure. And they never consider guards and servants human at all.

Presently, a fat man wearing crisp, white clothes walked up importantly to the door, he was carrying a silver box of paan and holding up the edge of his *antariya* like a dandy. He spotted me at the door and gave a puzzled stare, "You have been assigned to this office?"

I nodded. "I am assigned to the office of Ramadatta, officer of civil supplies."

"I am Ramadatta."

I bowed. He looked pleased. "So the minister does think I need a guard. I have been asking for one for quite a while, now that I am doing such important work." I bowed again. Ramadatta went in still smiling. It is nice when your spying actually pleases your quarry. It hasn't happened to me before.

After the auspicious beginning nothing happened for two whole days. There I stood for hours and hours, my calves knotting up with pain, my face splitting with yawns. Ramadatta was such an unbelievably boring man. I couldn't imagine spending my life doing what he did, day after interminable day. Bundles of official papers arrived at his office and he spent his days bent over page after leaf page full of notations about palace expenses, busily using his abacus to make his calculations about the cost of feeding the elephants or how many yards of cloth had to be ordered for curtains for a queen's chambers and so on. And he loved catching people out. One afternoon, I stood and listened to him bullying a palace cook who, according to Ramadatta was using too much *ghee* in his cooking. It was a ridiculous job.

It was ridiculous but I realised that it also did give him the opportunity to take bribes. There were all these people supplying things to the palace—cloth and carpets, vegetables and spices, furniture and flowers. All the orders for supplies had to be finally cleared by Ramadatta's boss, Minister Sripala, but the first check of the orders were made by Ramadatta. For a supplier it was essential to keep him happy. The problem was that, after listening in for two days to conversations about yards and seers, delivery dates and quality control, I did not hear a single word that could be linked to bribes. Ramadatta seemed to be a simple, rather jovial man who enjoyed his work and went home with an easy conscience. Contrary to what you may think, there are some people like that in this world.

On the third day, when I was close to giving up, things began to move. It was late afternoon, still too early for Ramadatta to stop work, when I noticed signs that he was closing shop. I had learnt his habits by now and grew alert when I saw him putting the papers away on shelves and locking up important bundles in a cupboard. He closed the desk, shut the windows and was reaching for his sandals, ready to leave.

"You are leaving early, sir?" I ventured.

He was looking nervous and excited, "Yes yes. I have some urgent work at home. Important visitors. You can go, too, if you want."

I had to move fast. I ran to a guard's cubicle, quickly changed my clothes, wrapped myself in a huge shawl so that I could hide my face and was at the gate in time to see Ramadatta walking away down the road. I followed at a safe distance, keeping my head well down and my shoulders hunched.

Ramadatta hurried on quite nonchalantly, without showing any sign that he suspected he was being followed. We entered one of the localities of Pataliputra where I knew many middle level bureaucrats like him lived. He walked quickly down the road and turned in through the gates of one house. At his knock, the door was opened by a maid and he disappeared inside.

I stood at the gate and gaped. This was no ordinary house, it was a mansion, the kind in which rich businessmen and high officials would live. Most of the houses in the lane were single storied and in the middle, this one towered to two tall stories. There was a high porch in front, the row of windows on the two floors draped with expensive curtains, a bird cage hung on the second floor balcony and the wooden main door was made of heavily carved teak. The house was spanking new, as a matter of fact, it was still not complete. I spotted some masons at work in the garden at the back, building what looked like a pavilion. Ah, my fat friend, I thought, you have to be on to some other source of income, your salary couldn't have built this.

Then it occurred to me that I was presuming too much without checking my facts, maybe Ramadatta did not stay here, maybe he was visiting. So I walked up to a cobbler sitting under a tree in the corner and asked," Tell me brother, who owns that house?"

"The fat man who went in just now."

"Must be rich."

The man shrugged. "He wasn't till some months ago. I have been sitting here for years. They had a small house, like the others in this lane. Then I heard he had inherited a lot of money from a relative. They began building what is turning out to be a small palace and the work hasn't stopped yet."

Inherited, sure. Minister Sripala had to be told about this. I realised I was oddly saddened by this discovery about Ramadatta. I had sort of begun to like the man. There was something genuinely friendly and simple about him. Or, it was a very good act.

I hung around across the road, hoping something would happen. He had spoken of visitors but no one had arrived so far. It was quite dark when the carriage drew up. A closed carriage, painted in some dark colour of maroon or blue. It came to a stop at the gate and the two men who alighted, held their heads down and hurried inside. I didn't like the way one man held a handkerchief to his face and nearly ran to the house. The door was opened immediately, as if the maid was waiting behind it, and the two men vanished inside. From my vantage point across the road, I hadn't been able to see their faces, all I could spot was that they wore good clothes.

I sauntered across to the carriage, the driver was brushing the horses down. "Good horses. Must have cost a packet to buy." The man went on with his work. "And a beautiful carriage too. Who owns it? Has to be an important man." I persisted.

The man turned to stare at me. "Very important, and it is none of your business."

I walked away before he got a good look at me. As I went past the carriage, I noticed a rather distinctive design painted on the side panel and wondered if I had ever seen it before. It looked like an emblem of some sort. I knew some official carriages had emblems like this but I couldn't place this one. It had that unmistakable official, royal look about it. The driver was still staring after me, so to calm him down I wandered off, turned the corner to get away from his line of sight and waited. I'm good at waiting, all spies are, we do our thinking while we sit and stare at empty roads and closed doorways.

So this was the way things were done, I thought, the negotiations and payments were made at home. It made my job that much harder. It was tough enough trying to catch a man taking a bribe at work but if all the transactions took place at his home, how was I to be there? Finding witnesses would be next to impossible. I was just deciding that I needed Sarvaka's advice on this, when the two men came out and got into the carriage, again, with their heads down, and at a galloping speed. Ramadatta had come out with them and bowed low in a very servile way as the carriage drove away. A stray thought came into my head, would a self-important bureaucrat bow like that to men who had come to bribe him? He was doing them a favour, wasn't he?

I looked around desperately for a carriage I could hire but this was a quiet, residential locality and none were around. I hurried behind the carriage and fortunately, once it reached the main road, the crowd of pedestrians and the growing evening traffic slowed its pace and I could follow on foot quite easily.

Pataliputra was getting ready for the evening and night's revelry and the roads were jammed with carriages, palanquins, bullock carts, horses, and people. Vendors had spread their wares on the pavements and buyers crowded around them and stray goats and cows made matters worse. The shopkeepers were lighting lamps at their doorways, and bunches of loud drunks were already lurking at the doors of the taverns. Swerving in and out of the traffic, skipping over puddles and open drains, I followed the dark carriage.

We reached the end of the busy bazaar and the carriage turned into a quiet, wide road and gathered speed. I ran after it for a while but lost it at one of the turnings, so I had no idea of which gate it entered. I looked around trying to get my bearings. This was one of the richest localities of Pataliputra. The lane was well lit and very quiet. The tall gates had guards behind them and long driveways led through gardens to the mansions. The houses were hidden behind banks of hedges and trees. Here a man like me would be watched with suspicion, so I walked away before any officious watchman came up to ask questions.

I was back in the safe noise and crowd of the bazaar, my head full of questions for which I had no answers. What had I got into? Ramadatta's friends were obviously rich and powerful men. But, I thought, wouldn't they be the kind who would go to Minister Sripala directly for their requirements, why bother to visit a junior official? In the three days I had watched him, Ramadatta never got a visitor who could live in a locality like this. I realised I needed the experienced head of my boss Sarvaka to worry through this puzzle.

I was close by Mallika's paan shop and wandered up. Now the shop was full of people. Mostly the rich and the idle young men who flirted with her for hours before buying the *paan*. Her *paans* were expensive, I suppose the cost of the back chat was also built-in and I must say, I did not see any of the young men complaining. They stood around, flower garlands wrapped around their wrists, eyes lined with kohl, smelling of perfume, and their lips reddened with the *paan* before they went to the houses of their mistresses or their favourite courtesan. Mallika was just a preliminary flirtation to get into the mood.

Once the crowd had lessened a bit I got closer and grinned, "Can an old friend get a *paan* free, beautiful lady?"

She handed me one. "How is your work going? I haven't seen you for days. They are keeping you busy."

"It is getting interesting. Today I saw some suspicious things though I don't know..." I shrugged.

"Ah! So the internal spying work can be interesting too, Kartik?"

As I nodded a bit reluctantly, Mallika sat back with a satisfied smile.

Chapter Two

Kartik Meets A Bureaucrat

Next morning, I decided to do some leg work. It would be a change from standing at a door, playing a guard and swatting the flies from your face. How can anyone spend his life just standing and staring into space, it's a mystery to me, really. The leg work was going to be checking out that lane past the main bazaar where I had lost the carriage the night before. I hated the idea of having to tell Sarvaka that I had lost it. Also, it was a sunny winter day and I was feeling quite energetic.

I had discarded my guard's uniform and instead, wore the clothes of a royal messenger, with the special red jacket and I carried a bundle of papers, tied with a string, that looked very important and official. It's a ruse I have used before, people remember the jacket not the face, not that my face is all that eye-catching. Going past the bazaar, when I entered the lane, it was still early and the sweepers with their lazy brooms were still raising a great fog of dust. I wandered up and down the lane twice, trying to spot if any house had a dark carriage parked inside, there were none that I could see. So it meant, doing a house-to-house check, going systematically down one side of the lane and up the opposite side, knocking on every door and telling my concocted tale.

I walked up to the gates or the main doors and once a guard or a maid came up, I asked if Minister Bhattaraka lived there and that I was carrying a message for him from the king. I had chosen the name very carefully and I was feeling quite pleased at my cleverness. There really used to be a Minister by that name, only he is the governor of a province now and does not live in Pataliputra any more. And if the face across the gate or at the door looked friendly, I tried to start up a conversation. Asking a maid for a drink of water, or sharing a *paan* with a doorman and then asking about the people who lived in that house.

It took me till noon to check out the dozen or so houses on both sides of the lane. It was a locality that was permeated with the smell of old money and had the cool detached air of the very rich. The kind that are so rich they don't feel the need to display their wealth. Just fastidiously keeping themselves away from riff-raff like me by staying behind high forbidding gates. There were a couple of retired generals, three noblemen, a prince who was a first cousin of the king and another who was his uncle. One of the richest courtesans of the city also had her home there with an attached music room and art gallery. Entry by invitation only, the gateman told me. Then at the second last house, just round the corner from the bazaar, I paused when I discovered that it belonged to Minister Sripala. Ah! Dear Kartik, I thought, my brain moving into high gear, this smells.

I needed to think. I wandered back to the bazaar and settled down at a food shop and ordered lunch. All the walking had made me ravenous and I can't think fruitfully on an empty stomach. Logically speaking, those men in the dark carriage must have gone into Sripala's house because it didn't look like any of the other residents of the lane could have anything to do with a senior clerk of supplies in the palace like Ramadatta. But Sripala met him at work everyday, why did Ramadatta have to go home to get a message from his boss? Also, if Sripala suspected Ramadatta of taking bribes, would he assign him a confidential job? And last night's clandestine action looked very confidential, indeed. The way those two men moved, it was positively sinister, as a matter fact.

The food shop man laid a banana leaf before me and ladled out the steaming rice, *daal*, and spicy vegetables. Sripala could wait, this was urgent. I was still munching when the man came back with second helpings. He smiled at my rapidly emptying plate. "All that walking's made you very hungry. I saw you going up and down the lane."

I nodded, not saying anything, my mouth was busy.

"You do eat fast." The man had a note of admiration in his voice. "You couldn't find the address you were looking for?"

I shook my head and then swallowed. "They must have got the address wrong at the palace. Just a waste of a whole morning."

"It's a quiet lane." The man sat down before me. "Not too many messengers or visitor's carriages come in during the day. The courtesan's nearly retired and only meets very select people and most of the others are old men. The only person who gets guests is a minister in the palace. A fat old man who lives there with his wife, son, and the son's family. I see him going to work every morning and the moment he is back home, the guests start arriving. The back of my shop looks into his garden and I see him receiving people from evening to late in the night. Must be an important man."

"Does he have a dark carriage? With an emblem on the side? I saw one just now."

"Nah!" The man grinned. "This is one bad tempered miser and he usually hires a carriage from the market and always argues with the driver over the fare."

By then I had finished eating and felt much revived. I paid the man with a tip and a compliment on his excellent vegetables.

The sun was high on the sky as I strolled along the bazaar. There is something about the markets of Pataliputra that always cheers me up. Though the questions pertaining to the case circled inside my head, I was also enjoying the colourful, busy bustle of the place. The women at the clothes and jewellery shops fingering the goods and haggling over the prices, the vegetable vendor calling out the beauty of his potatoes and brinjals, the man at the potter's shop loading a donkey with water jars and pots. The dust, noise, and the smell—that heady mix of horses' odour, cow dung and flowers, food, incense, wood, and earth. The yelling vendors merging their voices to the clatter of horse's hooves and carriage wheels. The high warning call of men bearing a palanquin, telling people to get out of their way. I stood for a while and listened to a magic-potion man singing out the unique properties of his powders that could cure everything from toothache to broken bones, stop hair loss, and even make your moustache grow. I laughed when he offered a medicine that would make me grow taller. I knew I was short and thin but it suited me. I had such a perfectly forgettable face—the most useful thing to have for a spy.

In the afternoon, I was back at my post at Ramadatta's door. That pesky guard at the next office wanted to know why I was late and I told him my grandmother was dead. She was, indeed, but died years ago. When people ask me too many questions I always make up the answers.

Late in the afternoon, Ramadatta called from inside and I went in. A big pile of papers sat on his table. "Would you help me carry these to the Minister's office please?"

"Yes sir." I said promptly. This was a great opportunity to start a conversation.

Laden with papers, I clumped on behind the fat behind of Ramadatta, down the long palace corridors of Ashoka's beautiful wooden palace. And all the while the man kept talking and I kept up an admiring echo. It wasn't easy I can tell you. This man really thought I would be falling apart with admiration for the fact that he had found a mistake in the costing calculation by the Fodder's Department for the royal stables. I mean, who cares how many bales of hay were munched up by Ashoka's horses? Maybe they were hungrier than usual. Then I heard about how he was now handling the work of a monastery being built and the king's travel programme, the expenses of the queen's quarters, and the royal kitchen. Ramadatta sighed happily as I exclaimed about the terrible burden of his work.

We got to Sripala's office and were made to wait in the antechamber. I took this time to look around. This man was really important. My boss Sarvaka had one clerk in his antechamber, this man had four. All guarding the door like obedient dogs and barking if you even went close. A stream of people went in and came out and there was a hum of anxious conversation in the inner room. Ramadatta went to sleep holding on to his precious papers while I sat and watched the people. We waited a long, long time.

As a matter of fact, we were the last to be called in and the inner room was emptying rapidly as the minister went through the last few petitioners. I looked at the man I had only heard about so far and not seen. One by one the people went up and bent over him and uttered their request in an undertone. The old man bent double to listen. Then he would call one of the clerks closer and whisper his instructions and the petitioner and the clerk would then hurry outside to finish the business. It was all very smoothly done and I could seldom catch more than a word or two of the conversation.

Then we went up to the low divan where Minister Sripala sat before a regulation-size, low table. He was a hugely fat, old Brahmin whose age could be anywhere from fifty to seventy, I wouldn't hazard a guess. The lines of his face were long lost in the layers of fat, the heavy dewlap of jowls waggling as he spoke. But if you thought this was a jolly fat man, you would be mistaken. The small mouth was always pursed in disapproval, as if he could detect a stink somewhere, and the beady eyes had a sharp, suspicious, oddly bitter glare in it. In all the while that we had been there, I had not seen him smile. But he did now, and it wasn't much of a sight, it was closer to a grimace of pain after a toothache starts hurting. Still, it pleased my fat Ramadatta, who was merely plump in comparison.

Nearly stammering in eagerness, Ramadatta explained his earth-shaking discovery as Sripala nodded absently. Then he said, "You have been very diligent Ramadatta. Leave the papers with me and I will take further action. I like your hard work."

Preening a bit, Ramadatta still had his doubts, "But sir, shouldn't I meet this supplier of hay myself? He has charged for nearly a third more than what he delivered and..."

"Leave it to me. I will sort this out." There was a sharp impatience to the reply. Sripala was obviously finding Ramadatta's eagerness a bit tiring. "This is an influential businessman and he has to be dealt with carefully. His brother-in-law is related to a prince. So, I think, I should deal with it."

Oh ho, I thought, the old game of the bureaucrats, pleasing the bosses and covering your backside at the same time. I was certain Sripala would do nothing to spoil his sweet relationship with the hay supplier, just obliquely let him know of what had happened and then a discreet little gift for the obliging minister would arrive at the next festival. Everyone will be happy and if Ramadatta knew the game he would stay quiet and get his share of the booty. As for the king's horses, being honest, dumb creatures, like most of us citizens, they wouldn't complain anyway.

My grandfather, who had seen this kingdom grow under the great Chandragupta, used to say that there is a special oil that all bureaucrats rub all over their bodies every morning. So everything unpleasant or inconvenient slips off. They can take credit for the good work of their juniors and please the royal family, and when things go wrong they remain untouched. My grandpa was not a polite man and used to say that if there is money to be made a well-oiled bureaucrat can slide through a sewer and come out smelling of jasmines. The secret was that oil and you can spot it in their smile. Sripala's ghastly smile simply oozed the stuff. As you can make out from my fulminations, unlike Ramadatta, I had taken a dislike to his boss.

What was making me even more suspicious was that he was being a little too sweet to Ramadatta, who was a subordinate, after all. Lots of smooth questions about Ramadatta's health, his wife's health, how his work was going... went on for quite a while. Then just as we were leaving, he bent forward and whispered something about appreciating what Ramadatta had done for him but I couldn't catch all the words. What was going on?

I decided this needed a more agile head than mine, I didn't know enough about the inner workings of the palace and so walked into my boss Sarvaka's office late in the evening and made a full report. He sat and listened in silence and then said, "It smells."

"Exactly my feeling."

"Either both of them are on the take or it is the minister and..."

"He is setting up Ramadatta to take the blame either way."

"But the big house, the carriage, your friend is showing signs of unaccounted wealth." Sarvaka thought for a while, absently scratching an ear and then continued, "This man Sripala is not much liked by people either. A bit of a troublemaker, tries to get in where he is not wanted. He's been trying for years to get into the inner circle of advisers to the king but somehow hasn't managed it as yet. Which is why when he asked me to check out that clerk I didn't take him too seriously."

"I know it doesn't count as much but I like Ramadatta..." I said tentatively.

"I don't like Sripala. Too oily for my taste." I was beginning to like Sarvaka, the man thought like me. " I think you should keep up the watch but now also include the minister. I am looking for corrupt officials and he is an official too."

"Yes sir!" I did like him. It was obvious that the fact that Sripala was a royal minister wasn't worth a pat of cow dung to Sarvaka and that pleased me inordinately. "This is now going to get interesting!"

He gave a sour smile. "His Majesty warned me that when you get involved things have a tendency to get interesting. So I was expecting this."

I shared his smile. "Nothing escapes His Majesty's eyes does it? He wouldn't be surprised by anything we discover about Sripala would he?"

"He wouldn't. But I'm not reporting to him until you get me something more concrete than the result of your over active imagination."

Feeling much better, light at heart, and hungry of stomach, I wandered into a nearby tavern for some food, wine, and the relaxation of inane conversation. The city was in its night mood. The taverns busy and noisy, the courtesans' houses blazing with light and swaying to music.

Men grouped at the street corners gossiped by the light of the torches, a few drunks tottered about and some even collapsed into the gutters.

At the tavern, the waiter got me some steaming fried meat and a jug of wine and I sat there relishing my food, thinking that working for Sarvaka may eventually turn out to be quite enjoyable. After a few bowls of the heady stuff, as I was beginning to feel particularly happy, I saw my old friend Lakshman come in. He is the head of a guild of woodcarvers. At my invitation he was happy to join my liquid celebration and he told me he had just come back from a trip to Rajgriha with an order for carved wood pillars for his guild.

"Rajgriha? What were you doing there?"

"Trying to become a supplier at a building site. The king is building a huge monastery there and I thought I would give it a try."

"Got a big order?"

"Not bad. It is a huge project and the king is supervising it personally. The main building is nearly complete but I have orders for some outer halls. I wasn't getting anywhere trying from Pataliputra but at the site, the architect was a fair man who liked the quality of the carvings on pillars that our guild does and put in the orders."

"It must be tough fighting the big businessmen in this city."

He nodded morosely into his winecup. "And they all have the officials in their pockets. I met one when this job was starting and realised I can't afford those huge bribes."

Through the haze of wine I remembered something Ramadatta had said as we were going to Sripala's office.

"Was the official who's handling the orders called Ramadatta?"

Lakshman shook his head, "No, this is a minister, a fat monster called Sripala."

"What did he say? How much did he ask for?"

"Oh, it was never as direct as that. He just talked about how poor he was and how he was planning to buy some land and how much that land would cost him. It was exactly a tenth of the order he was promising to me."

"But you can't say he asked for a bribe?" I grinned at him.

"Of course not. The poor man only talked of his dream of buying land in Pataliputra's best locality. It was his lifelong dream. So I said I was sorry I couldn't make his dreams come true and left."

"Must have broken his heart."

Lakshman laughed. "Sure. Only if he had one."

It had been a long and eventful day. With my head stewing in wine and whirling with crazy ideas, suspicions and speculation, I decided to totter home and go to bed.

Chapter Three

A Little Help from Mallika

Sarvaka had ordered me to keep watch on both Ramadatta and Sripala without any suggestion on how I was to do that alone. Cut myself in half? Find a ghost? Hire an assistant with my own money? That is, of course, typical of bosses. They are brilliant at coming up with clever, complicated orders but oddly absent-minded about how you are to carry them out. If he had to do the job himself he would get a taste of his own medicine.

So I was mumbling and grumbling to myself the next morning as I was trying to work out a new face for myself. I had decided to keep watch on Sripala for the next few days but the problem was that my old disguise would not work there because as a guard I would have to stand at the door of the antechamber and from there I would hear nothing useful. Also, I wanted to find a way to get inside his office, but a guard could never do that unless specifically called in for an errand. Sripala had seen me once already and that created its own problems. If I walked in dressed as, say, a messenger, he could wonder at the sudden change in my profession.

I sat before a polished brass mirror and brooded for a while, behaving a bit like an actor in a play. Then I oiled my long hair heavily and combed it differently, with a centre parting, making it flop over my eyebrows in slick strands. I also hoped the pungent smell of the hair oil would keep people at a distance. I put on a dirty old *antariya*, wrapping it around my legs, tied a torn piece of cloth around my head and then, as a final touch, pasted a false moustache over my lip. I was beginning to enjoy myself. I think, if I hadn't become a spy I would have wandered the provinces as an actor. I took a final look at my reflection, I looked poor, stupid, and because of the previous night's drinking bout, red eyed and a bit disreputable. Very different from the smart guard preening at Ramadatta's door. I looked just great, I thought with satisfaction.

My friend Kaushik came to my rescue again with an order for the guards at Sripala's door that I was to be let into the inside office to repair some broken wooden pillars. I posed as a carpenter from Lakshman's woodcarver's guild. Once while hiding from the police hunting for spies in a neighbouring kingdom, I had worked as a carpenter's assistant for a while and could manage to look authentic. One picks up the oddest of crafts while on the run—I can cook, weave baskets, make earthen pots and even sing a bit.

By the time Sripala bustled into his office, I had already been at work for some time and looked very busy surrounded by hammers, chisels, nails and wood shavings. He took one look at me and turned impatiently to one of the clerks who had followed him in. "Does this man have to work here today? He could work during the holidays, couldn't he?"

"One pillar is badly damaged, sir, and the man says he is not free after today, some work at the palace."

"His hammering will give me a headache."

"I'll hammer softly." I mumbled into my moustache, which was itching a bit.

Sripala sniffed with a pained glare on his jowled face, the fumes from my hair oil must have reached him. Then he gave me a suspicious second look as if my face had seemed familiar but thankfully didn't persist and in a moment was busy with his clerks, checking out the appointments for the day.

I was a very good carpenter because I worked very, very slowly. Have you ever seen a craftsman work fast? And I tapped softly with my hammer. So after a while Sripala had forgotten about me, proving my theory of the invisibility of guards, drivers, and servants correct again. All morning I studied a supreme bureaucrat at work.

There were three kinds of visitors coming to see Sripala—the important, the unimportant, and the forgettable. The first were the royal men, ministers, and big businessmen, who were ushered in immediately by a bowing clerk and Sripala got up from his seat to welcome them. The second were other officials, the junior ones, who had official work with the Minister, they were made to wait, entered laden with papers, and were spoken to in a brusque, business-like way, which was at the edge of rude disdain but never rude enough to be objectionable. The third were the poor, simple people, who came thinking that a minister of the crown was there to help them. Sripala pitied them for their illusions, made them wait for hours, at times never saw them all day, and spoke to them with an openly rude impatience that said that he was too important a man to waste his precious time meeting a potter or a flower seller praying that his bills be paid. These fools did not know the routine and actually expected their money without making Sripala and his clerks happy. The clerks gave them the real picture pretty fast. I realised something, everyone paid Sripala but it was so cleverly done, I would have a tough time proving anything.

A few times I managed to hear the instructions the clerks gave to the visitors. Payments were made at the homes of the clerks, so Sripala would never be caught taking any money himself. To catch the big man himself, I would first need a businessman willing to cooperate with me, then break the clerk into confessing, and then be there when the clerk was handing Sripala his share of the booty. Otherwise, it was just my word against his and who would believe a spy with oily hair?

There was another question that began to worry me after a while. Sripala had his gang in his clerks, then why was he involving Ramadatta? My fat friend was such a bad choice—he was not in the right place to be useful, he was too bumbling not to make mistakes, and he talked too much. The only reason could be that Sripala was covering his tracks in advance, in anticipation of trouble. Fat trusting Ramadatta was to take the blame if any suspicion fell of Sripala. There could be no other explanation.

The sound of jangling anklets made me turn from my pillar. A young woman was peeping in at the door with an enigmatic smile and then she said with a coquettish laugh, "Minister, can you spare a minute for a poor maid?"

Sripala looked up, gave his ghastly grin and waving her in said benignly, "Ah Raka! Come in! And how can the personal maid of Queen Mandakini be poor? I am always at your service, my child."

His child swayed in, looking very adult indeed. She was

in her twenties and a very conscious user of her pretty face and quick, dark eyes. She wore a diaphanous *antariya* tied with a lot of intricate pleats in front and a beaded *uttariya* flung across her shoulders. The hair was done up into a low chignon at the nape of her neck and decorated with flowers. The silver bangles and anklets were being jangled with great expertise and I had to give her credit for being able to flirt so convincingly with that ugly, fat, old man. Raka had come with a request from her mistress about getting some special silk. The traders coming by the 'silk route' from across the mountains had just arrived in Pataliputra with their bolts of the precious cloth and Queen Mandakini needed some for her puja room.

Queen Mandakini was one of the senior queens of late King Bindusara and I'd heard that the middle-aged lady was quite a power in the harem, the king often met her for her advice. So Sripala got very busy yelling for his clerks and personally noting down the order. I had stopped work to watch the action and during all the hustle and bustle, our child Raka found the time to look me over and we exchanged a smile. I must be a very handsome carpenter after all, oily smell and itchy moustache notwithstanding. As she left after some pretty thank-yous flung at the minister, she also managed to fling a quick look at me. I had a strong feeling Mallika would not like my newest conquest, I tried to imagine the look on her face if she had witnessed the scene and it made me grin happily.

By the time I had finished repairing the pillar it was way past my lunch time. So I gathered up my tools and wandered out to sit in the sun outside with my bundle of *chapattis* and vegetables. After a few hungry mouthfuls, I sat back and looked around and then froze. In the corner of the couryard a very familiar carriage with an equally familiar driver and two horses stood waiting. In the light of the day I studied it closely, it was the carriage that brought those two men to Ramadatta's home that evening.

It was painted a dark red with that distinctive emblem painted on the side panels showing an eagle under two flags. I decided to sit and wait till someone came out from the palace and left in the carriage. It was parked next to a gate leading out of the courtyard into the main palace area and so the owner of the vehicle could be in any of the offices around me or could have gone inside into the personal quarters of the royal family.

I was still sitting half an hour later when a soft feminine voice said somewhere, "Your work is finished for the day?"

I turned to see Raka standing behind me. She perched on the edge of a nearby verandah and gave me a smile that meant she had the time to chat. I nodded. "Nearly done, I only had to repair a pillar." I gave a smile that I hoped was nicely flirtatious. "You are a lucky girl, working in the palace."

"Mmm, it is easy work, the queen is a kind lady."

"But do you stay in the palace all the time or do you come out into the big, bad city sometimes too?"

She giggled. "What will I do in the big, bad city?"

"Do in Pataliputra? The delights of the city are endless! You could meet interesting people there. Much more interesting than that fat, ugly, old minister."

"Really? People like you?" And we shared a high pitched and a very false laugh.

All the while I had been keeping an eye on the carriage and now saw the driver go up to the gate and wait. I could see some men walking towards the gate, down the long cobbled pathway, skirting the next courtyard but they were still too far for me to see their faces.

"Who's come in that carriage?" I asked Raka. "Looks important."

"Prince Ketuvarman, he is a cousin of His Majesty, son of a step uncle or something like that." She shrugged. "He often comes to meet the queens, likes to keep the important harem women on his side."

"You don't like him?" She shrugged again but did not reply.

By now I could see the prince, a tall, dark, spare figure with the sharp bony features, which was typical of the Maurya clan, Ashoka looked like that, too. But what had robbed me of words was the sight of the plump man panting to keep in step with the long strides of the prince. It was Ramadatta and behind them, holding an umbrella over the prince's head, marched the troublesome and very curious guard from the next office who insisted on chatting with me everyday. I pulled an edge of my turban across my face, as if I was wiping my mouth, and kept sitting very, very still.

Ramadatta bowed the prince into the carriage and once the carriage had driven away, he hurried towards Sripala's office and disappeared inside, leaving the guard loitering at the door. I quickly gathered up my things. I had to get out fast before that guard looked around or Ramadatta came out again and they spotted me. If anyone in the palace could see through my disguise it was these two men and this was getting too close for comfort.

I kept my head down and somehow managed to continue with my inane chatter with Raka. Keeping her between me and the guard, I escorted her to the last courtyard of the inner palace, that led to the heavily guarded gates of the queens' quarters. I slipped through a side lane and rushed out of the office area and heaved a sigh of relief as I got to the main gate from where I could then vanish into the city crowd outside.

I walked around aimlessly for a while and then wheeled around and headed for Sarvaka's office. I needed to talk to a cooler head, also when it came to the royal family my knowledge couldn't possibly match his lifetime of gossip and personal experience. Now that a prince could be involved, I was getting a bit too anxious to calm down. Something like this may need a direct clearance from the king and only Sarvaka could get that.

As I trudged around the palace walls to the other end of the palace area where Sarvaka's offices were located, a stray thought kept nagging me. There was something that I was forgetting, a question that had begun to emerge when I saw the prince and his fat companion but then in the ensuing panic to avoid Ramadatta, I had lost the germ of the idea. Also, the remains of a hangover did not help. For about a dozenth time in my life I vowed to give up liquor.

There was no one available to hear my cry for help. Sarvaka was out of town, on a tour of the provinces and would only be back late the next day. His clerk had no instructions for me except that if I had a report to make,

I should wait till he came back and that I was not to do anything rash in his absence. The man had taken Ashoka's warning about me really seriously. So I went home.

If my mother was surprised to see her youngest son arrive in time for dinner she did not show it. She is not easily surprised anyway. I went into our small, tiled roofed home, washed my feet at the door, entered the inner courtyard and pulled a stool up to the bed where she sat working. She looked up from cleaning a *thali* of rice and said, "You are hungry very early tonight. Dinner is at least an hour away. There are some sliced cucumbers in the kitchen and some puffed rice in oil on the bottom shelf."

I came back with my snack and settled down beside her. "Do I only come home early if I'm hungry? Maybe I was missing you."

She laughed. It was the laugh of a mother of three sons, completely devoid of illusions.

"How is your work going? I met Mallika in the morning, she said you were working very hard and not moaning so much."

"Can't you two find any other topic to talk about except the state of my mind?"

"I want you to calm down and marry her before she changes her mind. No other girl will be foolish enough to have you."

"You found girls for all your other sons."

"I've found Mallika for you. Also, your brothers are sensible men, doing respectable jobs. Not looking like disreputable burglars with smelly hair." Ah! the hair oil. I grinned at her. "And if you have finished eating, go to the pond and wash off that muck from your head or you won't get any dinner." Then she gave a reminiscent smile. "Your father was just like you, coming home in the oddest of clothes. Once I mistook him for a milkman."

"If he had been alive, he wouldn't have ordered me to take a bath on a winter evening. I may catch a cold."

"Do you want dinner?"

I went.

After dinner I wrapped a warm *uttariya* around myself and went and sat on the back verandah, watching the night fall over Pataliputra. Our house is on a high patch of ground and on the edge of the road, so you look down into the city. Whenever I need to think, this back verandah is my chosen spot. The city was dark except for the flickering flame of torches lighted at street corners and the moving lamps inside nearby houses. I looked up at the clear, starry sky, it was nearly a full moon, a creamy ball of mellow *purnima* light.

Then it came back to me, that lost thread of thought. That morning when I had gone on a house-to-house check of the lane where Sripala lived, searching for the dark carriage, I had discovered that one of the truly palatial houses belonged to a member of the royal family. The name had meant nothing to me then, now it did—Prince Ketuvarman, cousin of our king. And he lived just half a dozen houses away from Sripala's. So, if the prince had some work wouldn't it be simpler to go to Sripala than send a carriage across town to Ramadatta's house?

My brain was now whirring on at great speed. Ramadatta was a junior official, he did not have the power to grant any requests. So whatever it was that Ketuvarman wanted would have to be eventually cleared by Sripala. My brain circled back to the first question that had come to me—if you belong to the royal family you go to the king with your requests, not lowly officials. So it had to be something Ketuvarman did not want Ashoka to know and also, he and Sripala were probably using Ramadatta as a mediator to create the impression that there is no connection between themselves.

I shook my head, feeling puzzled and confused, Military spying was so much simpler than this, there was never any confusion about who your enemy was. But this was like wrestling with shadows and I realised it was much harder than counting the cavalry strength of a rival king. I had this growing feeling that I was going into something too deep for me to handle and I needed Sarvaka near me. So cursing him for picking this time to go on his stupid tour, I went to bed.

Next morning I didn't know what to do. It made no sense guarding Ramadatta's door and the carpenter had no more legitimate work at Sripala's office. When I'm at a loose end there is always Mallika. So I offered her my scintillating company and I have to admit, she didn't look madly excited at the prospect of my services as a *paan* shop assistant for the whole day. Sometimes, she acts exactly like my mother.

I was leaning against the front of the shop when who do I see but my new friend, Raka the royal maid. She was wandering past the shops across the street, lazily checking out the wares on sale. Then she turned to cross the road and saw me. Quickly running through the traffic of carts and carriages, she came up to me with a breathless laugh. "I didn't expect to see you again!"

Feeling Mallika's watching eyes behind me, I produced my widest smile. "What a delightful surprise, lady Raka, I am truly honoured."

"Oh! And I don't even know your name!" And that eyelash-batting smile peeked out.

Mallika spoke, making Raka blink. "He is called Kartik."

Her quick glance now made the connection and then her delicate brows rose. "But you look different today, Kartik..."

"Ah, umm yes, of course... the moustache... I err shaved it off last night because..."

"I didn't like it." Mallika completed the sentence firmly, making herself very clear. "He looks better clean shaven, don't you think?" And she leaned forward to offer Raka a *paan* with a professionally smooth smile. And she had won. After a few more words, Raka wandered away chewing the *paan* with a disconsolate air.

I braced myself for the aftermath.

"So that is what is keeping you busy in the palace."

The only way I could save myself from the combined wrath of my mother and my girl was to make a complete confession and I told her everything. Mallika always knows when I am telling the truth. She listened very carefully to my report and then said, "What you need to do is get inside Ramadatta house."

"Not possible. He knows my face."

"I could try."

Sometime later in the morning, Mallika and I went loitering outside Ramadatta's house. He had already left for work by then and now we watched two women emerge from the door. A young woman carrying a basket of fruits and an older woman holding a *puja thali*. Both of them dressed in the cotton *antariyas* that women wear for worship.

"The younger woman is the maid, I saw her open the door that evening, so the older one must be Ramadatta's wife."

"They are going to the river for the *Kartik Purnima puja*." Mallika concluded, as we began following the two women. Then she wheeled into a nearby fruit shop, quickly bought a basket of bananas and green coconuts and was off behind the women, leaving me to follow as best as I could.

As I watched her in action, I decided that if I ever needed an assistant for my spying work I had one right before me. I sat on the crowded steps of the *ghats* at the bank of the Ganga river as Mallika settled down next to her quarry looking very devout. It was a sunny winter morning and the *ghat* steps were full of people who had come to worship. The air was filled with the chant of *mantras* and the cry of beggars and I sat and sniffed the fragrance of flowers and incense, feeling oddly contented, as I saw Mallika start a conversation with Ramadatta's wife.

By the time Mallika said goodbye to her new friend at the top of the steps, they were behaving like bosom friends. Ramadatta's wife was a soft faced, gentle—looking creature and she obviously liked talking because for most of the time, Mallika was nodding and listening. Once the two women were out of sight, I dragged her to a deserted part of the *ghat* and demanded a report.

"Anytime you want me to get inside that house just say so. I have a personal invitation from the lady herself."

"What was she telling you for so long?"

Mallika turned a thoughtful face towards me. "Kartik, you've got it all wrong. That house belongs to her. She was giving this special *puja* today because she had inherited money from her father and the house was finally complete. I liked her, she was telling the truth."

"How can you be sure?"

"Don't be stupid! Why should she lie to someone she's met at the river *ghat* and won't see again? Also, she was praying for her husband because he has suddenly been given important work and expects a promotion soon. She is convinced he will get it because a few days back a prince of the royal family came to their house. She has still not got over the excitement of the visit."

"So Ketuvarman went there himself that evening..."

"That's a simple and happy woman who is delighted with what is happening in her life, Kartik. She does not suspect anything wrong at all, I'm quite sure."

"I think you are right. It sort of fits with what I think of Ramadatta." I felt like hugging her but the *ghat* was too public a place. "You were brilliant."

She curved her eyes towards me. "Just praise won't do, I expect to be paid." That's my girl, businesslike to the last.

In the evening I went to Sarvaka's office again but he wasn't back. The clerk said he had been delayed and would only be back next morning. So I sat and chatted with the man and discovered that Sarvaka had gone to Rajgriha. I sat up at the name and began asking some more questions. It seemed the inauguration of the main monastery at Rajgriha was only a few days away. Ashoka was going bearing gifts for the monks and the main vihara. Sarvaka was checking out the travel route and security arrangements.

Why was Rajgriha cropping up everywhere around me? Ramadatta and Sripala are managing the supplies, Lakshman goes there, and now Sarvaka. I can never work out why but a few times in my life I have had an instinctive sense of impending danger and I trust the feeling completely. It has saved my life at least twice during my military spying days. Now that same feeling came back at this news about Rajgriha and the sense of danger was not for me but the king.

Walking home I decided that I couldn't wait for Sarvaka to come back, I had to act now. A plan was already crystallising in my mind and it was quite illegal and definitely not something I was allowed to do. So if Sarvaka wanted, he could sack me later for disobedience but the king had been very good to me and I owed this to Ashoka.

That night, after dinner, I went in search of a burglar friend of mine called Bhatti who had often helped me out of tight corners. I knew exactly where to look for him. For many years Bhatti had been passionately in love with a courtesan and spent all his free time and all his money at her feet. The courtesan of course had no objection to the arrangement and probably enjoyed his sharp company much more than the empty-headed, callow young sons of the rich who were her usual customers. Bhatti lived with the illusion that one day she would marry him and settle down to cooking his rice and vegetables.

The courtesan operated from a popular house of pleasure

and, as always, it was a busy place at night. I wandered through the courtyards where maids and waiters rushed about carrying wine jars and plates of food. The men loitered everywhere, wearing garlands and chatting to the women. Some of the courtesans eyed me invitingly from their doors or went past with a seductive laugh. You can always hear a courtesan approaching because of the elaborate *mekhala* belt covered with bells, that they wear around their waist. I threaded through groups of raucous men, bent eagerly over the *pasaka* boards, gambling. There was the sound of music, flutes and drums, anklets jangling, and female voices singing to loud drunken praise. This was Bhatti's world; I somehow never liked it.

Bhatti was at his usual spot in the corner, sitting over a jar of wine, munching fried gram. I sat down beside him and got a weary grin in welcome. He always looks exhausted, as if life is full of misery but you should see him run when being chased by a watchman. Bhatti moves like the wind. He has become quite a rich man now, with a shop in the market and burglary is, at times, more of a pastime. To my relief, he was not impossibly drunk yet and because of the crowd, he knew the love of his life wouldn't have any time for him that night, so a spot of burglary was quite fine by him.

We were going to enter Minister Sripala's house, without his invitation, of course, Bhatti as an experienced housebreaker knew that lane of the rich like the back of his hand. He worked out our route instantly. Before we went in, I told him what I was looking for, also, I made him promise that he wouldn't swipe anything from the house and that instead, I would give him a professional fee. When on the job he forgets and begins automatically picking up the silver and jewellery unless you warn him beforehand. I wanted to make sure that we left no trace of our presence inside. Sripala was too cautious a man not to take a burglary seriously. Whatever happened, I couldn't afford to let him go underground.

After skirting past the food shop where I had lunch that morning, we entered through the hedge in the back garden. It was a couple of hours past midnight and the house was in darkness. We crept through pillared halls with the dim shapes of furniture visible in the moonlight streaming through the windows. I was grateful that it was a full moon night or I would have stumbled over something. Bhatti moves with a silent, cat-like swiftness through it all and seems to have a sixth sense about sudden obstacles. He is familiar with the layout of such houses and as we entered the inner courtyard, he veered to the right to where he guessed Sripala would have his private study.

He was right. I closed the door behind me, then lit the lamp that stood on the low table and bent to look at the papers lying on it and on the divan. It seemed Sripala had been working late and had left all the papers out when he went to bed. I glanced quickly through the palm leaf bundles and then looked closely at larger sheets that had finely drawn diagrams and plans of some kind. Some of the sheets looked wet, the ink had still not dried on them and they had been laid out on the divan to dry.

Suddenly Bhatti bent down and blew out the lamp and dragged me towards the wall, his sharp ears had obviously heard a sound that I had not. We stood still and silent as I too, heard the footsteps of at least two people. A voice said outside, "I thought I saw a lamp in the study, the old man may have forgotten to blow it off."

The watchmen! The door creaked open and a head peered in. Bhatti and I were still as statues behind the door.

"No one's here and it's dark. Have you been drinking?"

"A little, it's cold brother..." and the footsteps receded.

We waited for what seemed like an eternity and then backed away softly through the courtyards, halls, the garden, and the hedge. I took my first full breath only when we were standing outside the food shop.

"Ooof! How do you do this, Bhatti? My heart was pounding so hard I thought those men would hear it. This is much scarier than spying!"

"It adds spice to life. I miss it if I stop, like wine or women..." Bhatti laughed. "You're sweating in this chill, Kartik! This was an easy job, they didn't even have dogs!"

Then Bhatti took his professional fee immediately, and in kind—a big meal at the most expensive food shop in town. He said he didn't trust me when it came to payment, spies are slippery customers, much worse than burglars.

Chapter Four

Kartik Declares War

ext morning, if Sarvaka was surprised to see me waiting for him at his office he didn't show it. But he must have seen something on my face because he waved me in at once, ordered the clerk to keep everyone away, took off his sandals and then settling down before his desk on the divan said, "You look anxious. Something's happened?"

"Too many things and I can't make any sense of it anymore."

He nodded and sat back against the bolster, ready to listen, and I began my report. It was concise and to the point, a bald statement of events in the right sequence and I kept all speculation out of it. I got it so perfect because I had spent most of the night before thinking of nothing else. Also I wanted Sarvaka to come to his own conclusions, optimistically hoping that maybe I was getting it all wrong. He listened in absolute silence, his eyes stilled on my face, holding back the questions till I had finished my story.

"So Kartik, what do you think is the truth?" His face was inscrutable and he still wasn't willing to reveal what he thought.

"If anyone is taking bribes and possesses property beyond his known sources of income it is Sripala. But it will take time to prove it..."

"And? There is something else, isn't there?"

"Yes." I took a deep breath and thought, here goes, "I think, the corruption of a minister of the crown is not what I have really uncovered. It's not even that important at this time. Sir, I can't give you one concrete reason but I think, this is something much bigger. There are too many unexpected happenings that don't add up to just a bribery scandal. What I saw in Sripala's house, the odd behaviour of Ramadatta, the sudden appearance of a member of the royal family..." Sarvaka raised his eyebrows in query. "I am worried about His Majesty's safety."

Sarvaka bent his head in thought and then said, "What exactly did you see on Sripala's desk last night? You just mentioned confidential papers."

"There were detailed architect's drawings of the new Rajgriha monastery and it looked like he had been copying them because there were roughly made copies with the ink still wet, drying on the divan. I didn't have enough time to study them closely but they seemed to be of the main vihara and the cells of the monks that are already complete."

Sarvaka looked quietly at me, watching my face as he said. "During the inauguration ceremony, three days from now, His Majesty will spend the first day in the *vihara* in prayer and discussion with the monks, followed by the inauguration, with the presentation of royal gifts the next morning and special chanting of prayers in the evening. So His Majesty will spend two nights there, staying like an ordinary monk in one of the cells and return to Pataliputra sometime the third day." He shook his head in an irritated sort of way. "This *vihara* is very important to him and he doesn't want to displease the monks. So he is refusing to listen to my suggestions about security and insists on a minimum of guards inside the vihara. The main contingents of the army has to stay outside in the town."

I sat completely silenced and stared at him in shock.

"No one knows the details of his programme except the *Agramatya*,—the Chief Minister, the *Dharma Mahamatra*,— the king's religious adviser who is a monk, myself, and Sripala."

"Why did Sripala have to know?"

"He organises the supplies for the king's entourage during the royal travels and so is given a copy of the king's programme."

"I saw the programme, too, on his desk last night, details of how many people are travelling to Rajgriha." I swallowed. "Including the army contingents."

Sarvaka nodded. "This is such a confidential matter that the programme is not to be shown to anyone or taken out of the palace. I keep mine locked in my personal safe."

I leaned forward, now it was my turn to ask questions. Just then the clerk poked his head in and said, "There is an urgent message from Minister Sripala's office. He wants to see you immediately."

Sarvaka stood up. "Ah! Our minister is getting anxious about something, summons so early in the morning is not his style." He turned towards me. "A talk with Sripala may clear my head. Don't go away." He began walking away and then said over his shoulder. "Good work, Kartik. We'll get to the bottom of this today."

"I want to be there to the end. You are not going to ask

me to stop, are you?" I wasn't going to let him take away the job from me now.

He turned and smiled slightly, "Of course not. And I even think in these circumstances that the burglary, though a bit reckless, was justified."

There is something to be said in favour of unburdening your fears. Feeling much easier in mind I came out of the office and sat under a tree in the park next to the courtyard, waiting for Sarvaka to come back. So far the only people whose praise had genuinely pleased me had been my parents and the king himself. But Sarvaka's last words had cheered me up to an inordinate degree and his condoning the burglary so casually made me smile.

Like Sarvaka said, Ashoka had the same attitude to important things, none of that strict obedience to rules even if it kills you, sort of nonsense that has always made my blood boil. I sat back and looked up at the branches of the *neem* tree and thought, this internal spying business has hidden shades and convolutions to it that are an unexpected pleasure. For all my worries about the king, I was actually enjoying myself.

The happy mood didn't last long because at the sound of horses I turned to look towards the avenue that skirted the park and saw the dark carriage coming towards me. It swerved away from the park and turned towards the quadrangle where Sripala's office was located. As it swept past I caught a glimpse of the beaky profile of Prince Ketuvarman inside. The prince did not seem to have anything to do except haunt the palace. I hoped Sarvaka had not come away from Sripala's office yet, I had a strong feeling the prince was headed that way. I got up and again took up my anxious post next to Sarvaka's door.

When he came back I followed him in and then he closed the door behind me.

"I saw the dark carriage, the prince was inside."

"He came in and joined us at Sripala's office." Now it was his turn to report. "The minister wanted a full report on the Ramadatta matter and I said we had our suspicions but no proof yet but that we were working on it." Sarvaka gave a faint smile. "He wasn't pleased and showed it. But that was not really the reason he had called me."

"What did he want to know?"

"Trying to sound very casual he asked me if His Majesty's tour of Rajgriha was final or not and if there were any last minute changes in the plans. Something that shouldn't concern him at all. He only manages the supplies, which should be in place by now anyway."

We stared at each other.

"I said I would only know this evening if the original programme stands and that was when Ketuvarman came in. I think he hadn't expected anyone in the office with Sripala so early in the morning. But he recovered very quickly and was very pleasant, trying to make small talk about the welfare of the king. But it was clear that Sripala was not pleased by his sudden appearance. He got rid of me pretty quickly after that."

"You'll have to brief me on Ketuvarman, I know nothing about him."

"I'll do it during the journey."

"Journey? Where are we going?"

"Rajgriha. The answer lies there and it is only a day's travel, we can be back by tomorrow evening." I am not bad at planning a strategy myself but this man's mind worked faster than mine.

"Shouldn't we tell the king?"

"Tell him what? That we suspect a *mahamatra* and his own cousin of planning some unknown crime but have no proof?" He was already on his feet. "I will only go to him with something more concrete than our suspicions, Kartik. You should know that Ashoka is not patient with jobs half done." Oh did I know about that! I knew exactly what Sarvaka meant. Ashoka was a fair king but not an easy going one. He liked things tied up neatly and if you wanted to come away safely from an audience, you had to be ready with all the answers.

Our carriage was galloping down the road to Rajgriha, the charioteer had instructions to go at speed and change horses regularly. Finally Sarvaka had the time to brief me on Prince Ketuvarman.

"He is a man who has always believed that he deserves more than what he has received. His father was King Bindusara's stepbrother but I think he believes he has a bigger right to the throne than Ashoka." He turned to give me a crooked smile. "Ashoka may have turned all holy now but he was ruthless when he claimed the throne. Ketuvarman realised he did not have a chance against a shrewd general like his cousin. During the battle for the throne, if you wanted to survive you didn't lay claims to the throne of Magadha and our prince Ketuvarman prudently stayed quiet."

"The maid Raka said he comes often to the palace."

"Yes, he has been trying hard to get into the good books of the king but Ashoka has not been too keen."

"It is the same story with Sripala. Our fat friend wants to be the king's chief minister."

"You can't misjudge Ashoka's instincts about people. I have never been able to pin the prince down but a few times when we have unearthed conspiracies against the king, Ketuvarman's name has come up. There is also some talk of his having squandered his inheritance and being in need of money, but I couldn't confirm it."

"But what are they planning?" I asked a bit fretfully, this uncertainty was getting me down. Sarvaka did not bother to reply. "If they try to harm the king, they'll regret it." Something in my voice made him turn and stare at me, "I'm declaring war."

"Good." And he closed his eyes and went to sleep.

We stopped for lunch at a small wayside inn where our horses were changed. I noticed a small two-horse carriage follow us in. Later in the evening, when our carriage was turning down a curve on the hilly road I happened to look back and the same carriage was right behind us. I pointed it out to Sarvaka and all he said was that it was a busy road with many people travelling to Rajgriha and that my head was full with sinister carriages.

Evening was falling when we swept into Rajgriha. It had once been the capital of Magadha and the high stone walls around the town still stood sentinel . Ashoka's new *vihara* was coming up in a large area and it was easy to find. The main *vihara* stood gleaming in the middle of all the construction work—piles of timber and stone, the dust, and the noise of the men at work. The path to the *vihara* was still being laid for the arrival of the king so we had to get off at some distance and walk the rest of the way.

This was my induction to a monastery—the place of worship for the followers of the Buddha. The buildings were laid out in huge quadrangles with cloisters and pillared galleries all around. The small spartan cells of the monks stood around courtyards with a *stupa* and the main prayer hall of the *vihara* in the centre. The image of the Buddha was in the prayer hall, where monks were always chanting prayers. The outer buildings, like the kitchen, bathhouses, and storehouses were still being built.

Sarvaka had been here quite a few times and was immediately admitted into the room of the senior most monk of the monastery—a thin, underfed, shaven-headed old man with such a serene, trusting face, I thought cynically that he wouldn't spot a conspiracy even if they dropped it in his lap. Still we asked a lot of questions about Ashoka's programme and Sarvaka was curious about the precious things kept in the monastery.

The old superior then called a young monk named Ratnapani and instructed him to take us to the main prayer hall where all the precious gifts were displayed. We followed the saffron-clad figure down endless corridors with carved wooden pillars and polished mosaic floors that echoed every slap of his sandals. Then we entered the prayer hall, walking down its long length, looking at the walls painted with murals of the Buddha's life, and went up to the huge statue of the great preacher.

I looked up at the tall, looming idol of Gautama Buddha, the stone figure of a man sitting in a meditative posture. The calm face had heavy lidded eyes and smiling lips, very different from the weapon-bearing gods and goddesses that Ashoka had once worshipped. In front of this peaceful figure, thin lines of smoke rose from bunches of incense sticks, rows of brass lamps glimmered in the gloom, and, the monks sat at the feet of their preacher, chanting *mantras* in a droning sing-song. I realised how quiet and serene this place was compared to our noisy, crowded places of worship.

Ratnapani turned out to be quite a talkative man as he showed us the prayer vessels of gold and silver, the jewelled bowls and salvers, boxes of precious spices, bolts of silk with the luxurious sheen of gold thread that had arrived from Ashoka. On the inauguration day, the king was going to present the biggest gift of all to the vihara—a relic of the Sakyamuni in a bejewelled gold box. According to Ratnapani, this relic was the most precious gift but to my burglar's mind, the jewels and gold seemed infinitely more tempting. I surveyed the gleaming pile before me, Ashoka was obviously trying to impress his new religious masters because there was truly a mountain of very rare and expensive treasures.

Ratnapani insisted we have dinner at the monastery. We were given a spartan meal in the refectory. Both Sarvaka and I stared in horror at the thin vegetable gruel in a bowl and dry pieces of chapatti bereft of *ghee*. The monks only eat once a day before noon so we were alone for this generous repast. After dinner, Sarvaka hurriedly told Ratnapani that we would find night's accommodation in town and that was a relief because if their cells were anything like their ideas on food I could face a pallet of grass on the floor.

Night had fallen as we bid goodbye to the friendly monk and picked our way through the rubble towards the road.

"So what do you think, Kartik?" Sarvaka asked, walking ahead of me.

"They want to steal the gold and silver or..."

"Do they want to harm the king?"

"Ketuvarman needs money and Sripala can never have enough."

"And Ketuvarman would like to be king."

We walked on in silence.

We were both walking with our heads down, and eyes focussed on the rough ground, trying to avoid tripping over it, when at a dark spot near a clump of high bushes, four men attacked us. Both of us carried daggers in our belts but we did not get the chance to reach for them as the men came at us, swinging their sticks. I ducked but then fell, reaching out desperately to clutch at the man's ankle as he aimed another blow at me. I managed to make him lose his balance but then he landed on me with bone crunching thump, pushing the last of my breath out of my lungs. As we grappled, someone took aim at my head and then everything went dark.

Head swirling dizzily, and a sick taste in my mouth, I slowly opened my eyes and discovered I was in a small earthen shack with a dim lamp flickering in the corner, filling the room with shadows. Holding my head I gingerly raised my bruised arms and legs to check if I could still move. They seemed to be working all right but there was a huge burning ache at my temples and my left wrist seemed to be broken. I turned to look around and saw Sarvaka lying very still beside me. My heart thudding with dread I reached down to feel his breathing. He had a gaping wound over one eye, the blood had dripped down and congealed on his face. He was unconscious, the blow had obviously knocked him out completely. To my relief, he was still breathing but I didn't like the sound of his soft groans.

I was thinking of getting up when I heard the rattle of someone dragging open the latch of the door. I promptly lay back and played dead. I could hear someone come in and then a voice said. "I think they are dead."

A second voice spoke, "We were told to kill them later anyway. So if they are dead already our work is done."

"Who gave you the orders, the prince?"

"Yes." The man laughed. "You don't think that fat minister would ever have the guts to order an execution do you? When I went in to report to Ketuvarman, he told me the minister has refused to come to Rajgriha fearing Ashoka will get suspicious. He'll only come after everything is over."

"What are we supposed to do with these two?"

"On the appointed night, we move into the *vihara* once Ashoka is inside. No one is to be left alive there. We set fire to it after the treasures have been carried away. The prince wants these two to burn too with their king. Our men followed them from Pataliputra and he says they were getting very close to discovering our plans. Just leave the bodies here. We'll collect them after the fire starts."

I lay there curled up on my side, still as death, listening to the men plan my funeral pyre, while praying that Sarvaka would not groan or move. To my relief he was still but that made me worry that he may have died. Then I heard the door close, the latch was pulled back with a rattle and I heard one man instruct a guard to stand outside and then their footsteps receded. With a groan, I struggled and sat up slowly and then I heard Sarvaka speak in a fading whisper, "So you are alive."

"Can you move?" He nodded. "There is one guard outside. We have to act now before the men come back."

When I tried to help him sit up I realised he was much more seriously wounded than I was. There was a deep stab on one thigh that made it very hard for him to walk, he couldn't possibly help me attack the guard. But he wasn't going to let me do it all alone. He dragged himself to the door and banged on it, yelling for help. Finally the guard opened the door, poked his head in saying, "Stop yelling! You are prisoners, you fools!" With a very authentic groan Sarvaka fainted at his feet. The man automatically bent down over him to look when I moved from behind the door and got to his throat. We are taught to kill swiftly and silently in the army.

I half dragged Sarvaka past the dead guard and we limped and groaned down the lane to reach the main road of the city where we managed to find some watchmen who we despatched to the monastery. It was dawn by the time the men came back with two litters for us, followed by an anxious Ratnapani and we were carried to the *vihara* where the monks were ready with their unguents and potions for our wounds. They must have given me something to sleep because when I woke up next, it was noon.

I limped over to Sarvaka's cell and found him sitting up, ordering the captain of the army contingent in Rajgriha to move immediately against Ketuvarman and his men who were holed up in a nearby estate. It was afternoon when the captain came back to report that they had surrounded and captured the prince's army but Ketuvarman had escaped and was said to be heading towards Pataliputra.

"Pataliputra? Why would he do that?" I asked puzzled.

"I think, he wants to get to the king before we can and somehow find a way to save his skin." Sarvaka drummed his fingers impatiently. "He'll try to pass on the blame to either Sripala or even try to prove that we were mistaken and attacked him needlessly. Or beg for Ashoka's forgiveness and I'm afraid he could get it too. The king is in a very pious mood nowadays. I've heard the prince talk, he can be a very persuasive man."

I got up. "You are too wounded to travel. Write a report for the king and I'll leave immediately for Pataliputra."

"Take that young monk with you, with a letter from the superior of the *vihara*. He'll make you sound more convincing."

I grinned. "I'm looking a bit too disreputable you mean?"

For the first time that day, Sarvaka smiled.

Chapter Five

A Report to King Ashoka

Chapter Five

A Report to King Ashoka

Still aching from the bruises and feeling a bit dizzy from the blow on my head, I climbed into the carriage and sat back with a sigh. Ratnapani climbed in after me and carefully stuffed a cushion behind my back and covered me with a warm blanket. I understood why he was travelling with me because I could imagine the sight I presented, covered in colourful bruises, with a bandaged head, strapped up wrist and a swollen eye. I looked like I was recovering from a drunken brawl. But Ratnapani, sitting next to me in the carriage speeding towards Pataliputra, was a portrait of caring holiness.

I told him so and he laughed. "You don't have a very high opinion of monks, do you? You'll be surprised to know that my father was a soldier who taught me to use a sword and I've not forgotten the skill. Our religion teaches peace but that does not mean we are weak. And neither is the king."

"Oh, I know Ashoka is strong but if you declare peace so loudly and publicly, even getting it carved on pillars that you plant across the kingdom, your enemies could get ideas and think of testing your intentions. I keep worrying that we'll be invaded. Then will his new faith let him go to war?"

He gave an impatient shake of his head. "Of course, he will. There are many kinds of war after all, Kartik." I stared at him with a quizzical look as he turned his sensitive face towards me, the large eyes studying my reactions. "The real war is against evil and you wage it both outside and within you. Marching armies, conquering lands where innocent people die, it is the war of conquest that Ashoka has given up. He will be just as energetic in defending his kingdom and his beliefs as before. This internal spying work that you are doing, isn't this a sort of war too? Just that the enemy is among us."

"I had never thought of it like that before." I said thoughtfully, making a discovery. "And I find I like this better than the marching armies. But it's a harder battle, much harder."

For all the wisdom in his words, he gave an oddly sweet, innocent smile, "I think you make a good warrior for peace, Kartik."

At all the stops on the road to Pataliputra, the wayside inns and small messenger huts where we changed horses, I asked questions and kept track of the entourage of Prince Ketuvarman. He was always a little ahead of us and that worried me, I was getting a bit obsessed about getting to Ashoka first. If both of us reached the palace at the same time he would definitely get an audience before me but when night fell we were still at least a couple of hours away from the city and I gave a sigh of relief.

"It's night! Perfect. Now he can't get to the king before us."

"Why not?"

"At nightfall the gates of Pataliputra are shut and you have to wait outside till the next morning. No one is allowed in, not even a prince, they only make an exception for Ashoka. So he'll still be sitting beside the moat when we get to the king."

"How can we enter the city if the gates are closed? You just said they won't open it for anyone but the king?"

I grinned, feeling truly happy. "No. But there are some advantages to being a spy, my holy friend. We do have some sneaky tricks up our sleeves."

Outside the city walls, in the countryside, there are openings to tunnels that take you under the walls and inside Pataliputra. Only the senior spies know about them and we would lose our lives if we revealed their locations to anyone. Ashoka, like his grandfather Chandragupta, never really stops being a king and he likes to be kept informed all the time. He has given instructions that the reporters and informers, whenever they arrive, are to be taken to him instantly. During expeditions, I have reported while he was having his bath, in the harem, and even once when he lay injured and the physicians did not want him to be disturbed. I knew that once I got to the palace, he would see me.

Leaving the carriage outside, we entered an innocuous looking building and I led Ratnapani down the stone steps and into the tunnel. We walked along the narrow, bricked passage, holding our torches high before us. It smelled of damp and of furry creatures, moles and rats, and it felt as if there was not enough air for us to breathe. We walked on in complete silence and only when I had raised the trap door at the other end and we emerged in the open air, did we take long breaths and smile at each other in relief. I have always disliked walking through the tunnels and the monk obviously felt the same.

We had emerged at the outskirts of the city, in an area full of orchards and gardens, and walking out on to the road, I hailed a horse cart that took us to the palace. Ratnapani said this was his first experience of the city at night and obviously the sights of Pataliputra quite dazzled him. I did not go directly to the palace but took a quick detour to a small house nearby to pick up Kaushik. I fed him a short version of the latest happenings, as he sat beside me, sleepily tying on his turban. I knew Ashoka would need him next to go after the culprits, including my good friend Sripala.

With Kaushik beside us, we had no problem getting past the palace gates and drove swiftly through the outer quadrangles to the inner gate of the king's personal palace. The door was blocked by the guards as one of them went running to get the chamberlain. As we stood impatiently, hugging ourselves and stamping our feet in the late night chill, the royal chamberlain, a huge fat eunuch came walking leisurely towards us. I have had many late night battles with this personage before while trying to get to Ashoka with a report. He believed himself to be a very superior being and thought the main purpose of his life was to guard the king from riff-raff like me. For him the king's sleep was more important than the news of an invasion. So I knew what to say.

"Greetings Chamberlain! This is Kartik, Cara first class, Kaushik, captain of the palace guards, and His Holiness Ratnapani, a senior monk at the Rajgriha vihara. We need an immediate audience with His Majesty about a matter of great urgency." I felt Ratnapani turn and stare at me when I gave him such a high rank but wisely, stayed silent.

The old eunuch wheezed through the bars of the gate.

"But His Majesty is sleeping! He cannot be disturbed at two in the morning."

"This is important, you fool!" Kaushik began to lunge forward in rage but I held him back. Aggression does not work with this slow thinking palace puppet, only fear of Ashoka's wrath does.

"Then we'll wait, Chamberlain." I kept my voice cool, "but tomorrow if His Majesty is angry at the late arrival of the report I will have to inform him that it was because his loyal chamberlain was protecting his royal sleeping hours."

The door creaked open and we were let in. I heard Ratnapani stifle a laugh.

We walked quickly down the corridors of the palace, dimly lit by sputtering torches, and reached the door of the king's bedchamber. Ratnapani and I handed the letters from Sarvaka and the *vihara* superior to the chamberlain of the royal bedchamber and waited. Within minutes we were summoned inside.

Ashoka was sitting up in bed holding the two letters. We three bowed low as he gave an impatient wave and said, "Talk, Kartik." My heart was thudding as I began my report. I kept my eyes on the king's face trying to read his reaction to my words but in the dim, flickering light of the night lamps, all I could see was his sharp, beaky nose, the firm sculpted lips, and those shadowed, deep-set eyes that did not leave my face for a moment. Even in his abruptly awakened state, with untied hair and dishevelled night clothes, this was my king and if I mixed up my report he would get my head.

When I came to a breathless stop, he turned to Kaushik, "Do you have anything to add?"

Kaushik came forward, "My guards have reported the frequent meetings between Prince Ketuvarman and Ramadatta and also some early morning and late night visits of the prince to Minister Sripala's office. Yesterday the minister's clerk told me that Sripala plans to leave for Rajgriha tonight. We need to move immediately, Your Majesty, before the gates open and the prince gets to the minister."

"Do you have anything to say, Bhikshu?" The king now looked at Ratnapani.

"The prince has visited Rajgriha quite a few times recently, though he does not live there." Ratnapani added. "Last month, he visited the *vihara* and at his request, I took him around the site and he asked a lot of questions about the building plans and the number of people living there. I did find his questions a little odd, Sire, as he showed no interest in our work or the teachings of the Buddha."

Then things began to move at lightning speed. Still sitting up in bed, Ashoka rapped out about half a dozen orders and suddenly the whole palace was in an uproar. The chamberlain and his band of slaves rushed about, lamps and torches were lit, messengers sped off with summons for the Crown Prince, the Chief Minister, and senior army generals. Then Kaushik vanished with a bunch of men to get Ramadatta, another group was despatched in search of Sripala and one general and his men went marching off to the city gate to capture Ketuvarman.

Ratnapani and I retreated to a corner of the king's

bedchamber, pulled up two low basket seats and sat back tiredly, leaning against the wall. The two of us could finally take some rest. In our mad rush to the city, we hadn't even stopped to eat and I was aching all over and weary to the bone.

Then a slave came up to us with a tray of food. "His Majesty said you two look very hungry and, sir, the royal physician is on his way to tend to your injuries."

Ratnapani looked up in surprise as Ashoka, who was at the other end of the room, still in his night clothes, pacing about in conference with a general, called out to us, "You two stay here and rest." His craggy features split in that typical, knowing grin, "And Kartik, how do you manage to get beaten up so regularly?"

I grinned back happily, nothing escapes his eyes. I have always marvelled at the way he can balance the role of a king, with his inherent kindness. He really is remarkable. Sometimes I wonder, if he is truly human, tough, decisive, at times even ruthless but also oddly vulnerable, and a caring man. And that is why, he is my king.

I was tired but that did not mean I was going to miss any of the action. Ratnapani had no intention of going anywhere either. So we resisted the offers of warm beds and instead, settled down with some cushions and blankets in the outer room, next to the king's bedchamber and kept an eye on the arrivals. The hot food was like ambrosia and then a physician came and tut-tutted over my wounds and put some cooling unguents on them that eased much of the pain. We two sat there, watching the movement around us, like two actors in the wings whose roles were over in a play.

Kaushik was the first to arrive with a Ramadatta shivering with fear and Ashoka came out to question him. He called me over and I went and stood nearby. The king had changed into his royal clothes, a deep red *antariya* and a warm tunic on top, with a thick *uttariya* wrapped around him against the early morning chill. His hair was now tied in a turban and gold and jewels glittered at his throat, ears, and arms. He was going to look right when he faced his cousin. He sat down on his royal seat in the audience room, surrounded by the Crown Prince, the Chief Minister, and the senior most army commander and then to my surprise, he ordered me to take a seat, pointing to a cushion at his feet.

After a few questions it was quite clear to everyone in the room that Ramadatta was an innocent man. He guilelessly recounted how some months back Sripala told him that he had been chosen for important palace work and that it was highly confidential. So every few days he acted as a courier between the minister and the prince, at times carrying letters home that Ketuvarman's men came and collected. Also, Sripala had kept a close watch on all the work at Rajgriha and Ramadatta was told to bring along all papers on the *vihara* work the moment they arrived. Then Ramadatta pulled out another letter saying that Sripala had wanted it to be delivered to Ketuvarman the day before but he discovered that the prince had suddenly left the city.

Ashoka read the letter and then handed it to me. At a first reading it seemed like an innocuous missive but then I realised that Sripala was confirming the king's programme at Rajgriha was unchanged and that Ketuvarman could move as planned. Ramadatta fell at the king's feet, blubbering with tears, begging to know what he had done wrong, he had believed he was only working for the king. After a stern lecture about the foolishness of trusting too blindly, Ashoka told Kaushik to take the weeping man away, explain what was going on and let him go. I gave a small sigh of relief.

I was still sitting at the king's feet, playing a reluctant acolyte, when almost simultaneously Ketuvarman and Sripala were brought in. The two men met at the door and exchanged a glance that dripped with venom. What followed was a familiar scene of falling-out among crooks. Each blaming the other, each claiming innocence, while the roomful of people listened to them in silent disbelief.

The conspiracy was exactly what Sarvaka and I had surmised. Ketuvarman wanted to be king and Sripala's ambition was to be the chief minister of Magadha. They had been looking for an opportunity for a long time and when Sripala discovered Ashoka's intention of spending time in the *vihara* as an ordinary monk with a minimum of security, they spotted their chance. The *vihara* was going to be attacked at night, all its inhabitants including the king killed, the treasures looted, and then the buildings were to be set on fire. Ketuvarman said it was all planned by Sripala and he was only going along to discover his plans and then as a loyal subject he would have revealed it all to the king. I had to admit he had worked out a convincing tale during his trip from Rajgriha. Then Sripala whipped around and screamed his innocence and said actually he was the loyal one and then mentioned how he had started an enquiry against the renegade clerk

Ramadatta, and both of them looked a bit startled when we all laughed.

Ashoka leaned forward and his voice was cold, "So both of you are loyal to me. I wonder who could be the real culprit? Maybe that poor fool Ramadatta. He must have planned it all alone and used you two loyal, innocent men."

Finally the two men fell silent as the king waved an angry, impatient hand and the two were taken away. As he was getting up from his seat, Ashoka put his hand on my shoulder for a moment and said, "Kaushik will send a carriage and a physician to get Sarvaka. You can go home." And then as I bowed before leaving, there was a touch of sadness in his eyes, "It is good to know there are some people I can trust, Kartik."

Bursting with pride, like someone had put a medal around my neck, I went home. My mother and Mallika would be waiting.